Children's Books:

Mr. Getaway and
The Christmas Elves

Sally Huss

ISBN: 0692339450
ISBN 13: 9780692339459

We were back in school after our Thanksgiving break

When we got the news that our teacher had a bad tummy ache.

The word was that she had eaten too much turkey and pumpkin pie.

This sad news should have made us cry.

But not for long because we knew we were in for a treat

With Mr. Getaway as our substitute

Who knew what adventures we'd meet.

"Get your coats and your hats, Class. We're on our way,"

Called out the bold and exciting Mr. Getaway.

We bundled up and jumped on the bus

Not knowing where we were going or where he was taking us.

It would be better than sitting in a classroom

Working on subtraction and multiplication.

We were going on a field trip with an unknown destination!

Mr. Getaway, in his usual shrewd style,

Wouldn't tell us where we were heading, just hinted with a smile.

"At this time of the year," he asked,

"What in all the world would you like to see?"

Goodness, I thought, could it possibly be?

Is it Santa's workshop that he's taking us to see?

The bus headed north and my heart began to pound.

No one had ever been there,

No one had stepped on that hallowed ground.

Then the bus slowed and passed through

Some snow-covered trees

And there was a sight of which any child would be pleased.

There were elves running around, up and down, here and there

And none of them was paying us the slightest attention,

Not the slightest care.

They were busy as busy as you can imagine them to be

With Christmas coming, there was non-stop activity.

Mr. Getaway had to explain things to us,

"Stay out of their way! This must be a must."

We could watch them. We could study them.

We could see what they do.

But we could not distract them whatever we do.

This was the rule that we had to obey.

We had to promise or we just couldn't stay.

You'd think that having such a strict rule for their guests

Might indicate peace and quiet, and some orderliness.

But not so! The place was a jumble of action, even chaotic,

It seemed to me

With elves running everywhere as far as the eye could see.

They were working feverishly creating mounds of toys

That would be placed under trees for good girls and boys.

Surprisingly enough, as hard as they were working

On each of Santa's elves there was a happy smile lurking.

They seemed to be happier

Than I'd ever seen anybody work before,

Happier than any of my classmates

Who thought working was a bore.

They danced and twirled and did flips and sang

While working alone, in pairs or in gangs.

They were putting faces on dolls…

And putting air into balls.

Some were attaching tubing to bicycle wheel rims

And some were painting trains or dollhouse door trims.

Others were putting together an electronic device.

While another was adjusting a telescope

That had to be most precise.

There were endless gobs of books that needed labels

And teeny, tiny hooks that needed to be put on jewelry stacked

On teeny, tiny tables.

No detail was left undone

On any toy that would give any child great fun.

To make these gifts seemed to delight the elves

And they were making rows and rows of them

On shelves and shelves.

The more they made the happier they got.

This was indeed an unusual lot.

For not one of them got to play

With any of the toys that they made that day.

Fortunately, Mr. Getaway shed some light

On what we thought for the elves was not right.

He said, "An elf takes delight in the work that he does.

It is his way of sharing his love."

"You might say that love is care

And you can see that there is abundance

Of care everywhere."

Then he pointed to a sign on the wall.

It was something that would touch us all.

It read: Work is wise. Work is good.

It makes us happy to do more than we should.

No wonder the elves were enjoying what they were doing.

That's why none of them was complaining or stewing.

Then all of a sudden the commotion came to a halt

And at the end of the room a great door opened

Like the lock on a vault.

And whom do you think appeared in that space?

Yes! Yes! It was Santa with his great whiskered face.

He spoke to us briefly, "The elves work hard all year through

Without a word of thanks for all that they do.

They have discovered the secret to happiness…

Which I hope you will all learn

Which is to give without asking for anything in return.

Hmmm… Now you may be wondering what do I do

All the rest of the year

When I am not riding my sleigh and reining in my reindeer?

I live far off in the great golden sun

And I send out small, invisible gifts everyday to everyone.

They are carried on the backs of the sun's glorious rays.

These are special gifts to make you stronger and happier

As you go through your days.

So now that you've finished your visit, get back to school

You've done very well. You've followed our rule.

I'm sure that the elves' work will find a place under your tree

And remember when you look at the sun, think of me."

Oh my, we all sighed as we got back to our seats

This was a special outing full of treats upon treats.

Mr. Getaway waved and smiled that day as he left the classroom.

We all hoped, as always, that he'd be back soon.

Then we got back to our studies and books

And there was not one frown, no grumpy looks.

We had learned a lesson that we shall never forget

From one day's outing that we will never regret.

It is that doing something for others is more important

Than all the gold it might bring.

It is the only thing that will make your heart truly sing!

The end,
but not the end
of working happily.

At the end of this book you will find a Certificate of Merit that may be issued to any child who honors the requirements stated in the Certificate. This fine Certificate will easily fit into a 5"x7" frame, and happily suit any child who receives it!

Here is another charming and whimsical book by Sally Huss.

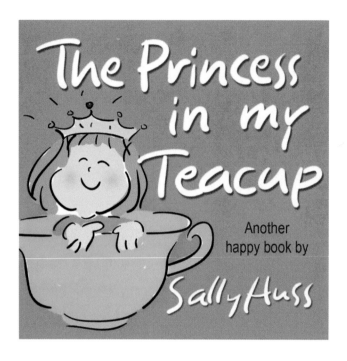

Synopsis: What little girl would not want a princess to visit her? That's what kept happening to the little girl in this story. A princess would show up in a mud puddle, the kitchen sink, a bathtub, and even in a cup of tea. But it is what the princess told her that was most important, and the little girl took it to heart. Who was that princess in her teacup? You'll have to read the book to find out.

All in rhyme and accompanied by over 35 delightfully colorful illustrations that dance along with the story.

THE PRINCESS IN MY TEACUP may be found on Amazon as an e-book or soft-cover book -- http://amzn.com/B00NG4EDH8.

If you liked MR. GETAWAY AND THE CHRISTMAS ELVES, please be kind enough to post a short review on Amazon by using this link: http://amzn.com/B00PVEXA8Y.

You may wish to join our Family of Friends to receive information about upcoming FREE e-book promotions and download a free poster – The Importance Happiness on Sally's website -- http://www.sallyhuss.com. Thank You.

More Sally Huss books may be viewed on the Author's Profile on Amazon. Here is that URL: http://amzn.to/VpR7B8.

About the Author/Illustrator

"Bright and happy," "light and whimsical" have been the catch phrases attached to the writings and art of Sally Huss for over 30 years. Sweet images dance across all of Sally's creations, whether in the form of children's books, paintings, wallpaper, ceramics, baby bibs, purses, clothing, or her King Features syndicated newspaper panel "Happy Musings."

Sally creates children's books to uplift the lives of children and hopes you will join her in this effort by helping spread her happy messages.

Sally is a graduate of USC with a degree in Fine Art and through the years has had 26 of her own licensed art galleries throughout the world.

This certificate may be cut out, framed, and presented to any child who has demonstrated her or his worthiness to receive it.

Certificate of Merit

_____
(Name)

The child named above is awarded this Certificate of Merit for working happily at home and in school, and for promising to be:

*Generous whenever possible
*Helpful to others
*Friendly to everyone

Presented by: _____   Date: _____

Printed in Great Britain
by Amazon.co.uk, Ltd.,
Marston Gate.